P9-CFF-397

An I Can Read Chapter Book™

# The Battle for St. Michaels

Emily Arnold McCully

HarperCollinsPublishers

*For Anna Loughridge*



The Battle for St. Michaels

www.harperchildrens.com

Library of Congress Cataloging-in-Publication Data
McCully, Emily Arnold.
The battle for St. Michaels / by Emily Arnold McCully.
p. cm.
"An I can read Chapter book."
Summary: In 1813, nine-year-old Caroline, a fast runner, helps the residents of St. Michaels, Maryland, as they defend their town against the British.
ISBN 0-06-028728-4 — ISBN 0-06-028729-2 (lib. bdg.)
1. United States—History—War of 1812—Juvenile fiction. [1. United States—History—War of 1812—Fiction. 2. Running—Fiction. 3. St. Michaels (Md.)—History—Fiction.] I. Title.
PZ7.M13913 Bat 2002 2001039814
[E]—dc21 CIP
AC

1 2 3 4 5 6 7 8 9 10

First Edition

# Contents



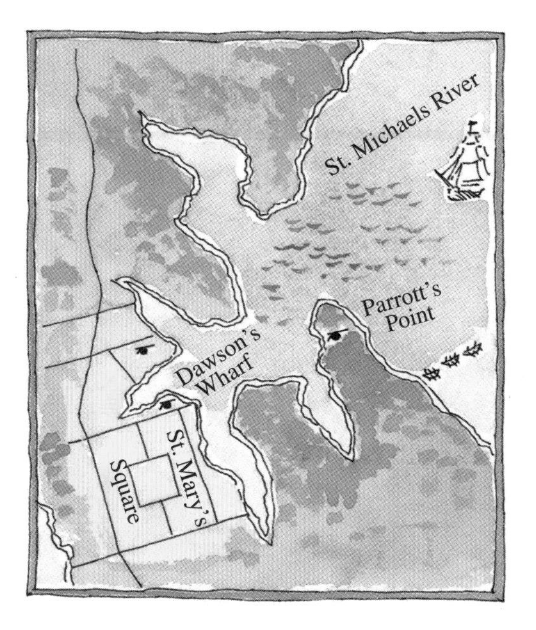

St. Michaels River
Parrott's Point
Dawson's Wharf
St. Mary's Square

# Chapter One

*August 8, 1813 – 10 A.M.*

The town of St. Michaels was preparing to defend itself against the British navy. British ships came closer every day, and soldiers from the Maryland militia had filled the town.

Caroline and Robert were watching the soldiers drill at the wharf. Suddenly a scout ran up and reported alarming news.

"I must tell my mother what has happened!" Caroline cried.

"Wait for me, Caroline," Robert called.

But Caroline ran ahead of him. She was faster than Robert. In fact, at nine and a half, Caroline Banning was faster than anyone else in town under fifteen.

Soldiers seemed to be everywhere these days. Six of them were staying at Caroline's house. It was a scary time in St. Michaels—but it was exciting, too.

“Mother!” Caroline cried as she and Robert burst into the kitchen. “The British navy has burned the town of Havre de Grace to the ground!”

“Dear heaven! Those poor people!” said Mrs. Banning.

“They say the British stole the clothes off the backs of women and children,” Caroline said.

“I hope the British show up here,” Robert said. “They will learn how the men of St. Michaels fight!”

“If they attack us, there will be little we can do,” Mrs. Banning said.

"Do you think St. Michaels is truly in danger?" Caroline asked.

"I pray not, child," her mother said. "If Havre de Grace burned, St. Michaels surely could."

"I don't want St. Michaels to burn!" Caroline said.

“We have cannon,” Robert said. “We can defend ourselves!”

“Robert, you don’t know what war is really like. You have caught war fever from men who should know better,” said Mrs. Banning.

"We fought the Revolution for our liberty. You don't want the British king to take it back, do you?" Robert asked.

"I wish Papa were here!" Caroline said. Her father had been away for four months defending Fort McHenry, in Baltimore.

"I wish he were here, too," her mother said. "But we must keep our heads—and prepare."

# Chapter Two

*August 8 – Midday*

Later that day, Caroline and Robert went to Parrott's Point, where Captain Dodson was in command. He was Caroline's father's best friend. Caroline wasn't used to seeing him in uniform.

"Caroline," he said, "shouldn't you be at home helping your mother? This is hardly a place for children."

Caroline blushed. "We wanted to see the cannon that will defend St. Michaels," she said.

"I have to admit I'm glad you're here," said Captain Dodson. "I have an urgent message for Captain Kemp in town."

“Sir, I will take it to him!” Robert cried.

“Caroline is faster,” Captain Dodson said. He handed her the note.

Caroline ran the mile and a half to town in a flash. Captain Kemp read the note and quickly wrote a reply for her to take back.

"Good work," Captain Dodson said when she returned. "Now go on home."

"But I want to help," said Caroline.

"You already have," Captain Dodson said. "And your father would want you to be looking after your mother."

Caroline did as she was told, but she would rather have stayed.

At home, old Mr. Clapton was visiting. He had fought in the Revolution.

Mrs. Banning was saying, "Last week we heard the British were going to attack Wade's Point. But it was just a rumor. Maybe they won't attack St. Michaels, either."

"Sooner or later there will be a battle," said Mr. Clapton. "The British know this is a ship-building town. They want to burn the new ships in our harbor so our navy can't use them."

Caroline said, “I was just at Parrott’s Point with Captain Dodson. He has a cannon there to defend us.”

“His cannon won’t hold off the British,” the old man said. “They have an entire fleet loaded with guns.”

“Robert says their navy isn’t brave like ours. He says a lot of their sailors have deserted,” Caroline said.

Mr. Clapton said, “They are still brave enough to burn the whole town and fly their British flag over the ashes of St. Michaels.”

# Chapter Three

*August 9 – Afternoon*

The next day, Caroline and her mother made the soldiers' beds, scrubbed, and dusted. For once, Caroline was glad to do the chores. They made life feel normal. She could believe that nothing bad would happen to St. Michaels.

Later, Robert came to the door.

"You're to come to the town square right away for a meeting," he said. "One of the general's scouts saw a British ship headed for the harbor! And there were more ships behind it!"

Caroline and her mother hurried to the square. Most of the townsfolk were already there. The general called them to order.

"We've captured a British deserter. He says they intend to land this very night," the general said.

The crowd gasped. Caroline looked around at their faces.

"Women and children are to leave town and take anything of value," he said.

Caroline grabbed her mother's arm. "Can't we stay?" she whispered. "I want to help! I can run messages."

Then the general turned to Mrs. Banning. "Madam, I must ask you and a few others to remain in town to give housing to my soldiers. Your child can go with Mrs. Dodson."

"No!" Caroline cried.

"I need her help," Mrs. Banning said.

"Very well," said the general. "But be prepared to flee at a moment's notice. We may not be able to hold the British off."

"I couldn't bear to send you away now," Mrs. Banning whispered to Caroline.

People hurried in all directions, boarding up their windows and loading wagons. The town was coming apart.

Caroline and her mother hid their silver tea set and china, a necklace, and Caroline's French doll in a barrel in the basement. Then they covered the barrel with straw.

"The redcoats will never find these," Caroline said.

"You had better pack clothes. We might have to leave quickly," her mother said.

Fog had rolled in, and a misty rain started. A wagon rumbled past.

*What if we never see our neighbors again?* Caroline wondered. *What if St. Michaels is burned to the ground?*

Mrs. Banning stroked Caroline's hair. "It's getting late," she said softly. "I wonder if the soldiers will want supper."

Suddenly a soldier appeared out of the mist. “We’re meeting at the church,” he said. “The general says to bring coffee and food—and to hurry!”

# Chapter Four

*August 9 – 8 P.M.*

The general and his officers looked out of place in the church. Robert and a few other boys sat in a back pew. Caroline handed out cups of coffee. She was proud to be at the important meeting, too.

"The stormy weather favors us," the general said. "It's harder for the British to attack when they can't see the town."

"But they can shoot cannon from the ships in the harbor even if it rains all night," a man said.

"And if they do, there will be fires," Mr. Clapton added.

“We will hold them off as long as we can,” said the general. “And as long as we do, we will keep the Stars and Stripes flying over St. Michaels.”

Then someone spoke up. "I've heard that at night, ships sometimes hang lanterns at the tops of their masts. When enemies see the lanterns, they aim at them, thinking they'll hit the ships. But the lanterns are so high, the shots fly above the ships, doing no harm."

Everyone started talking at once.

"Order!" the general shouted. "Fooling the redcoats may be our best hope. Keep your houses dark and hang lanterns in the trees and on the rooftops and the masts in the harbor. With a bit of luck, the British will shoot at the lights, and the balls will sail right over the town!"

There was a cheer. "People who aren't here must be told," someone cried.

"You boys in the back, tell the plan to people in the houses on the hill and run lanterns up the trees," the general said.

*Boys!* Caroline looked at Captain Dodson. He saw her and nodded. "You, too, Caroline," he said. "You are the fastest."

Caroline ran out to the main street. She dashed from house to house, banging on doors. "Put out your lights!" she cried. "Hang lanterns on your roof! We must fool the British tonight!"

Only old Mr. Wade protested. "What foolishness is this, child?" he asked.

"Please!" Caroline cried. "It's our only hope!" She explained the plan.

He rubbed his chin and said, "It just might work. I will do it."

All over town, lights were put out and lanterns shone near the rooftops. Caroline and the boys climbed tree after tree, tying lanterns to the highest branches. In the thickening fog, the town seemed to rise into the sky.

Caroline and Robert walked together toward the square.

"It's so dark now," Robert said. "Are you scared?"

"I don't know," she said. "I haven't been thinking about it—I've just been telling people the plan."

Robert didn't have a chance to say how he felt. Just then Captain Kemp called to Caroline and handed her a note. "Run your fastest to Parrott's Point. Get this to Captain Dodson!" he said.

# Chapter Five

*August 9 – 10 P.M.*

The night was silent. Caroline could hardly see two feet in front of her. Somewhere in the gloom, the British fleet lay in wait.

Losing her way only once, Caroline reported to the captain. Robert arrived as he was reading the message.

"The redcoats are in the Eastern Bay," Captain Dodson said. "We have only our cannon to stop them from landing."

Caroline looked up at the flag. She knew that Captain Dodson, like her father, had sworn to defend it with his life.

"Caroline and Robert, it isn't safe here. But I may need to send you for help. Will you stay?" Captain Dodson asked.

"Yes, sir!" they said. Caroline and Robert looked at each other. They were going to help defend St. Michaels!

The company of men, thirty in all, sat in small groups around the cannon. Most were silent, for fear their voices would carry out over the water.

"I wish I had a musket," whispered Robert. "Or even a bayonet!" He looked on the ground for a long stick.

They waited and waited. Caroline grew sleepy.

John Stevens, one of the soldiers, said, "Maybe this will be like Wade's Point. They manned the cannon all night there, too. The landing never happened."

"Maybe nothing will happen tonight, either," Caroline said.

Then the silence exploded.

# Chapter Six

*August 10 – 3 A.M.*

*C-R-A-C-K!*

It was a musket shot. The men snapped to attention. In the next instant, Caroline heard clipped voices nearby. Footsteps sloshed over wet ground.

Suddenly she could see rows and rows of redcoats plunging out of the mist.

There had been no warning at all.

Caroline stood frozen. All around her, the townsmen watched in horror as the enemy advanced on them. Then the men began to run toward town.

Only Captain Dodson and John Stevens stayed. “Hold the flag!” the captain shouted, pushing it into Caroline’s hand. Robert had vanished.

The two men wrestled with the cannon, trying to fire it. Finally, it blasted into the night.

"Retreat!" Captain Dodson shouted. "Caroline, save the flag!"

Caroline bolted.

Moments later, she heard the redcoats give three cheers of victory.

Caroline was trembling so hard, she nearly ran into a tree. She kept imagining the redcoats charging forward. She'd been right in the thick of battle! But there was no sound of anyone following her. She was safe. She hoped that Captain Dodson and John Stevens were safe, too.

She heard musket fire from the harbor. The men of St. Michaels were fighting back!

Caroline hurried toward town.

Suddenly, there was a sickening boom—she knew at once what was happening. The British ships were firing cannons on St. Michaels!

# Chapter Seven

*August 10 – Dawn*

Caroline ran to her house.

"Oh, Caroline, I've been so worried," her mother cried.

"Parrott's Point was overrun. I saved the flag!" Caroline said.

The cannons continued to boom.

Caroline told her what had happened.

"Thank goodness you're safe," her mother said. She looked at the flag. "Your father will be proud of you."

"Saving the flag won't matter if they burn the town," Caroline said.

"There are no fires yet," Mrs. Banning said.

Finally the cannons stopped. Morning arrived, but the thick fog hid the sun.

There was a knock at the door. It was Captain Dodson.

“You’re safe!” Caroline cried.

“And so is John Stevens,” he said. “Our trick worked. The British overshot the town. The only roof hit was old Mrs. Merchant’s. The cannon ball followed her down the stairs but did no other harm.”

"No one was hurt?" asked Caroline.

"Not a one!" he said. "But not all were as brave as you. Thanks to you, our flag will fly proudly again and all will see that St. Michaels is safe."

"I was scared," Caroline admitted.

"You were right to be," Captain Dodson said. "We were barely spared last night."

People were coming out of their houses, waving and calling to one another.

Robert saw Caroline. "Over three hundred British marines landed on Parrott's Point!" he said. "I ran when I saw them. But you didn't."

"I felt like running, too," Caroline said. "But Captain Dodson needed help."

"I never want us to be attacked again," Robert said. "But if we are, I hope I am brave enough to stay and help, too."

"Caroline," Captain Dodson called, "come run the flag up the pole. Show everyone the battle for St. Michaels is over!"

# Author's Note

During the War of 1812, American attempts to invade Canada spurred the British to retaliate with attacks on Maryland towns along the Chesapeake Bay. St. Michaels, home to the clipper ship, was one such target.

On the night of August 9, 1813, more than three hundred British troops landed on Parrott's Point, where an American cannon was positioned to protect St. Michaels. Overwhelmed, all the defenders fled except Captain Dodson and a freedman named John Stevens. They were able to fire the cannon once before also fleeing. With the cannon no longer a threat, the British returned to their ships and launched a barrage of firepower at the town.

Many years after the war was over, sons of Captain Dodson and Captain Kemp claimed that using a pirate trick had warded off the cannonade, and St. Michaels became known as the town that fooled the British and saved itself. Today, some historians think the tale of hanging lanterns in trees and on roofs is just a legend. What is certain is that when the fog lifted in the morning, St. Michaels had survived the attack.

While Captain Dodson, Captain Kemp, and John Stevens were all real people, I created Caroline, her mother, and Robert to imagine what it might have been like to participate in a desperate attempt to use trickery to save a town.